Edgar Allan Poe's

TALES of MYSTERY and MADNESS

To Roger Corman and Vincent Price, my childhood nourishment of Poe,
and special thanks to Caitlyn Dlouhy, for her strength and endurance, and to
Mr. Crab Scrambly, for helping me keep my head above water.
—G. G.

Atheneum Books for Young Readers
An imprint of Simon & Schuster Children's Publishing Division
1230 Avenue of the Americas New York, New York 10020
Text abridgment copyright © 2004 by Simon & Schuster, Inc.
Illustrations copyright © 2004 by Gris Grimly
Book design by Kristin Smith
The text of this book is set in Locarno.
The illustrations are rendered in pen, ink, and watercolor.
Manufactured in China
11 12 13 14 15 16 17 18 19 20
Library of Congress Cataloging-in-Publication Data
Poe, Edgar Allan, 1809—1849.
Edgar Allan Poe's tales of mystery and madness /
Edgar Allan Poe ; illustrated by Gris Grimly.
v.   cm.

Contents: The masque of the red death—Hop-Frog—
The black cat—The fall of the house of Usher.
ISBN 978-0-689-84837-7
1. Horror tales, American. 2. Children's stories, American.
[1. Horror stories. 2. Short stories.]
I. Soenkson, Stephen, ill. II. Title.
PZ7 .P7515Ed 2004
[Fic]—dc22   2003010565
1012 SCP

Edgar Allan Poe's
TALES of MYSTERY and MADNESS

illustrated by

Gris Grimly

Atheneum Books for Young Readers
New York London Toronto Sydney

CONTENTS

The Black Cat

For the most wild yet most homely narrative I am about to pen, I neither expect nor solicit belief. Mad indeed would I be to expect it, in a case where my very senses reject their own evidence. Yet, mad am I not—and very surely do I not dream. But tomorrow I die, and today I would unburden my soul.

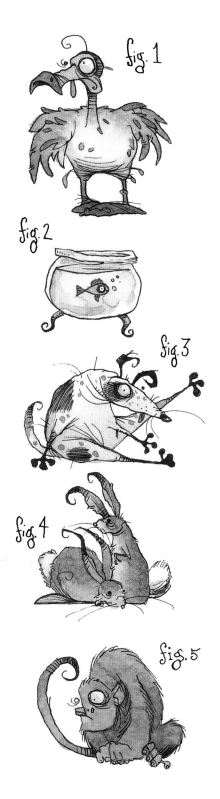

fig. 1

fig. 2

fig. 3

fig. 4

fig. 5

From my infancy I was noted for the docility and humanity of my disposition. I was especially fond of animals, and was indulged by my parents with a great variety of pets. With these I spent most of my time, and never was so happy as when feeding and caressing them. This peculiarity of character grew with my growth, and, in my manhood, I derived from it one of my principal sources of pleasure.

I married early, and was happy to find in my wife a disposition not uncongenial to my own. Observing my partiality for domestic pets, she lost no opportunity of procuring those of the most agreeable kind. We had birds, goldfish, a fine dog, rabbits, a small monkey, and *a cat*.

This latter was a remarkably large and beautiful animal, entirely black, and sagacious to an astonishing degree. Pluto—this was the cat's name—was my favorite pet and playmate. I alone fed him, and he attended me wherever I went about the house.

Our friendship lasted in this manner for several years, during which my general temperament and character—through the instrumentality of the Fiend Intemperance—had experienced a radical alteration for the worse. I grew, day by day, more moody, more irritable, more regardless of the feelings of others. I suffered myself to use intemperate language to my wife. My pets, of course, were made to feel the change in my disposition. I not only neglected, but ill-used them. For Pluto, however, I still retained sufficient regard to restrain me from maltreating him. But my disease grew upon me—for what disease is like Alcohol!—and at length even Pluto began to experience the effects of my ill temper.

150 ml

XXX

est. 1832

One night, returning home much intoxicated from one of my haunts about town, I fancied that the cat avoided my presence. I seized him; when, in his fright at my violence, he inflicted a slight wound upon my hand with his teeth.

The fury of a demon instantly possessed me. I knew myself no longer.

I took from my waistcoat a penknife, grasped the poor beast by the throat, and deliberately cut one of its eyes from the socket!

When reason returned with the morning, I experienced a sentiment half of horror, half of remorse, for the crime of which I had been guilty; but it was, at best, a feeble and equivocal feeling, and the soul remained untouched. I soon drowned in wine all memory of the deed.

In the meantime the cat slowly recovered. The socket of the lost eye presented, it is true, a frightful appearance, but he no longer appeared to suffer any pain. He went about the house as usual, but, as might be expected, fled in extreme terror at my approach. I had enough of my old heart left as to be at first grieved by this evident dislike on the part of a creature which had once so loved me. But this feeling soon gave place to irritation. And then came the spirit of PERVERSENESS. Who has not, a hundred times, found himself committing a vile or stupid action, for no other reason than because he knows he should *not*? The spirit of perverseness, I say, came to be my final overthrow. It was this unfathomable longing of the soul *to vex itself*—to do wrong for the wrong's sake only—that urged me to continue and finally con-summate the injury I had inflicted upon the unoffending brute.

One morning, in cold blood, I slipped a
noose about its neck and hung it to the limb
of a tree; hung it with the tears streaming
from my eyes, and with the bitterest remorse
at my heart; hung it *because* I knew that it
had loved me, and because I felt it had given me
no reason of offense; hung it *because* I knew that
in so doing I was committing a sin—a deadly sin
that would so jeopardize my immortal soul
as to place it even beyond the reach of
infinite mercy.

On the night of the day on which
this most cruel deed was done, I was aroused
from sleep by the cry of "fire." The curtains of my
bed were in flames. The whole house was blazing. It was
with great difficulty that my wife and myself made our escape.
The destruction was complete. My entire worldly wealth was
swallowed up, and I resigned myself thenceforward to despair.

I am above the weakness of seeking to establish a sequence of cause and effect, between the disaster and the atrocity. But I am detailing a chain of facts—and wish not to leave even a possible link imperfect. On the day succeeding the fire, I visited the ruins. The walls, with one exception, had fallen in. This exception was found in a wall, not very thick, which stood about the middle of the house, and against which had rested the head of my bed. The plastering had here resisted the action of the fire—a fact which I attributed to its having been recently spread.

About this wall a dense crowd was collected, and many persons seemed to be examining a particular portion of it with very minute and eager attention. I approached and saw, as if graven in *bas-relief* upon the white surface, the figure of a gigantic *cat*. There was a rope about the animal's neck. When I first beheld this apparition, my wonder and my terror were extreme. I went so far as to regret the loss of the animal, and to look about me, among the vile haunts which I now habitually frequented, for another pet of the same species, and of somewhat similar appearance, with which to supply its place.

One night as I sat, half stupefied, in a den of more than infamy, my attention was suddenly drawn to some black object, reposing upon the head of one of the immense hogsheads of gin, or rum, which constituted the chief furniture of the apartment. It was a cat—a very large one—fully as large as Pluto, and closely resembling him in every respect but one. Pluto had not a white hair upon any portion of his body; but this cat had a large, although indefinite, splotch of white covering nearly the whole region of the breast.

11

Upon my touching him, he immediately arose, purred loudly, rubbed against my hand, and appeared delighted with my notice. This, then, was the very creature of which I was in search. I at once offered to purchase it from the landlord, but this person made no claim to it—knew nothing of it—had never seen it before.

I continued my caresses, and, when I prepared to go home, the animal evinced a dispositon to accompany me. I permitted it to do so, occasionally stooping and patting it as I proceeded. When it reached the house, it domesticated itself at once and became immediately a great favorite with my wife.

For my own part, I soon found a dislike to
it arising within me. This was just the reverse of
what I had anticipated, but its evident fondness for
myself rather disgusted and annoyed me. By slow degrees
these feelings of disgust and annoyance rose into the bitterness
of hatred. I avoided the creature; a certain sense of shame, and
the remembrance of my former deed of cruelty, preventing me
from physically abusing it. But gradually I came to look upon
it with unutterable loathing.

1.

EXHIBIT A

2.

EXHIBIT B

3.

EXHIBIT C

What added, no doubt, to my hatred of the beast, was the discovery, on the morning after I brought it home, that, like Pluto, it also had been deprived of one of its eyes. This circumstance, however, only endeared it to my wife.

With my aversion to this cat, however, its partiality for myself seemed to increase. It followed my footsteps with a pertinacity that would be difficult to make the reader comprehend. Whenever I sat, it would spring upon my knees, covering me with its loathsome caresses. If I arose to walk, it would get between my feet and thus nearly throw me down, or, fastening its long and sharp claws in my dress, clamber to my breast. At such times, although I longed to destroy it with a blow, I was yet withheld from so doing, partly by a memory of my former crime, but chiefly—let me confess it at once—by absolute *dread* of the beast.

This dread was not exactly a dread of physical evil—and yet I should be at loss how otherwise to define it. I am almost ashamed to own—yes, even in this felon's cell, I am almost ashamed to own—that the terror and the horror with which the animal inspired me, had been heightened by one of the merest chimeras it would be possible to conceive. My wife had called my attention, more than once, to the character of the mark of white hair, of which I have spoken, and which constituted the sole visible difference between the strange beast and the one I had destroyed. The reader will remember that this mark, although large, had been originally very indefinite; but, by slow degrees—which for a long time my reason struggled to reject as fanciful—it had assumed a rigorous distinctness of outline of a hideous—of a ghastly thing—of the GALLOWS!

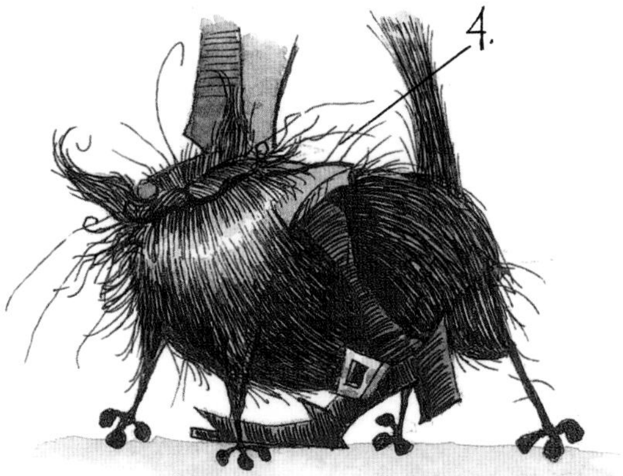
4.

EXHIBIT D

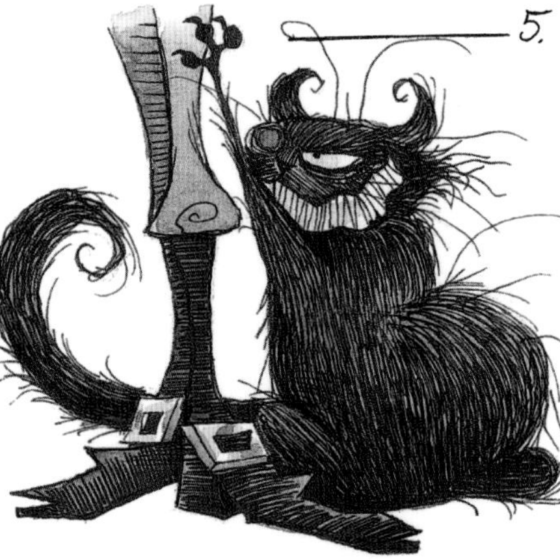
5.

EXHIBIT E

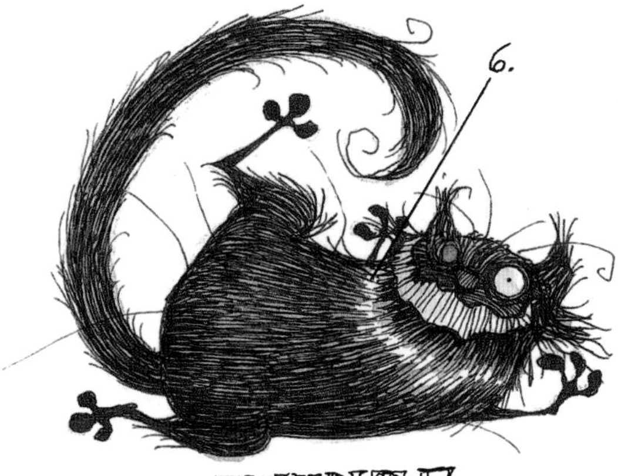
6.

EXHIBIT F

AND NOW WAS I INDEED WRETCHED BEYOND THE WRETCHEDNESS OF MERE HUMANITY.

Alas! neither by day nor by night knew I the blessing of rest anymore! During the former the creature left me no moment alone, and in the latter I started hourly from dreams of unutterable fear to find the hot breath of *the thing* upon my face, and its vast weight—an incarnate nightmare that I had no power to shake off—incumbent eternally upon my heart!

Beneath the pressure of torments such as these, the feeble remnant of the good within me succumbed. Evil thoughts became my sole intimates—the darkest and most evil of thoughts. To sudden, frequent, and ungovernable outbursts of fury to which I now blindly abandoned myself, my uncomplaining wife, alas, was the most usual and the most patient of sufferers.

One day she accompanied me, upon some household errand, into the cellar of the old building that our poverty compelled us to inhabit.

The cat followed me down the steep stairs, and, nearly throwing me headlong, exasperated me to madness.

Uplifting an axe, and forgetting in my wrath the childish dread which had hitherto stayed my hand, I aimed a blow at the animal which, of course, would have proved instantly fatal had it descended as I wished. But this blow was arrested by the hand of my wife.

Goaded by the interference into a rage more than demoniacal, I withdrew my arm from her grasp and buried the axe in her brain. She fell dead upon the spot.

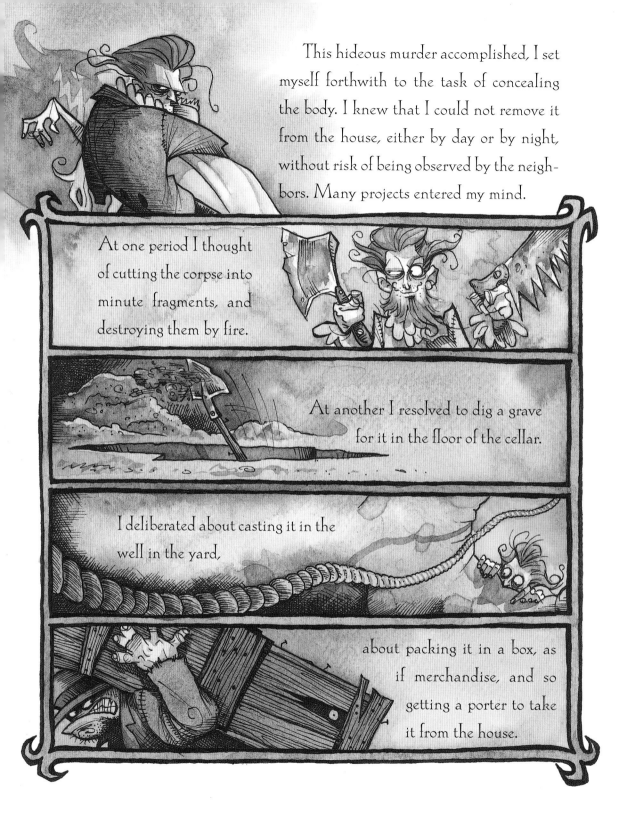

This hideous murder accomplished, I set myself forthwith to the task of concealing the body. I knew that I could not remove it from the house, either by day or by night, without risk of being observed by the neighbors. Many projects entered my mind.

At one period I thought of cutting the corpse into minute fragments, and destroying them by fire.

At another I resolved to dig a grave for it in the floor of the cellar.

I deliberated about casting it in the well in the yard,

about packing it in a box, as if merchandise, and so getting a porter to take it from the house.

Finally I hit upon what I considered a far better expedient than any of those. I determined to wall it up in the cellar, as the monks of the Middle Ages are recorded to have walled up their victims.

For a purpose such as this the cellar was well adapted. Its walls were loosely constructed and had lately been plastered throughout with a rough plaster, which the dampness of the atmosphere had prevented from hardening. Moreover, in one of the walls was a projection, caused by a false chimney, or fireplace, that had been filled up and made to resemble the rest of the cellar. I made no doubt that I could readily displace the bricks at this point, insert the corpse, and wall the thing up as before, so that no eye could detect anything suspicious.

In this calculation I was not deceived. By means of a crowbar I easily dislodged the bricks, and, having carefully deposited the body against the inner wall, with little trouble I relaid the whole structure as it originally stood. Having procured mortar, sand, and hair, with every possible precaution, I prepared a plaster, which could not be distinguished from the old, and with this I very carefully went over the new brickwork. When I had finished, I felt satisfied that all was right. The wall did not present the slightest appearance of having been disturbed. The rubbish on the floor was picked up with the minutest care.

My next step was to look for the beast which had been the cause of so much wretchedness, for I had, at length, firmly resolved to put it to death. But it appeared that the crafty animal had been alarmed at the violence of my previous anger, and forbore to present itself in my present mood. It is impossible to describe, or to imagine, the deep, blissful sense of relief that the absence of the detested creature occasioned my bosom. I soundly and tranquilly slept; aye, *slept*, even with the burden of murder upon my soul.

The second and third day passed, and still my tormentor came not. Once again I breathed as a free man. The monster, in terror, had fled the premises forever! I should behold it no more! My happiness was supreme! The guilt of my dark deed disturbed me but little.

Upon the fourth day of the assassination, a party of police came, very unexpectedly, into the house.

Secure, however, in the inscrutability of my place of concealment, I felt no embarrassment whatever. The officers bade me accompany them in their search. They left no nook or corner unexplored.

At length they descended into the cellar. I quivered not a muscle. My heart beat calmly as that of one who slumbers in innocence.

I folded my arms upon my bosom, and roamed the cellar easily from end to end.

The police were thoroughly satisfied and prepared to depart. The glee at my heart was too strong to be restrained. I burned to say but one word, by way of triumph, and to render doubly sure their assurance of my guiltlessness.

"Gentlemen,"

I said at last, as the party ascended the steps,

"I delight to have allayed your suspicions. I wish you all health and a little more courtesy. By the bye, gentlemen, this—this is a very well-constructed house."

(In the rapid desire to say something easily, I scarcely knew what I uttered at all.)

"These walls—are you going, gentlemen?—these walls are solidly put together"

—and here, through the mere frenzy of bravado, I rapped heavily with a cane that I held in my hand upon that very portion of the brickwork behind which stood the corpse of the wife of my bosom.

But may God shield and deliver me from the fangs of the Arch-Fiend! No sooner had the reverberation of my blows sank into silence than I was answered by a voice within the tomb!

A cry, at first muffled and broken, like the sobbing of a child, and then quickly swelling into one long, loud, and continuous scream, utterly anomalous and inhuman—a howl— a wailing shriek, half of horror and half of triumph.

Of my own thoughts it is folly to speak. Swooning, I staggered to the opposite wall. For one instant the party on the stairs remained motionless, through extremity of terror and of awe. In the next, half a dozen stout arms were toiling at the wall. It fell bodily.

The corpse, already greatly decayed and allotted with gore, stood erect before the eyes of the spectators. Upon its head sat the hideous beast whose craft had seduced me into murder, and whose informing voice had consigned me to the hangman. I had walled the monster up within the tomb.

The Masque of the Red Death

The "Red Death" had long devastated the country. No pestilence had ever been so fatal, or so hideous. Blood was its avatar and its seal—the redness and the horror of blood. There were sharp pains, and sudden dizziness, and then profuse bleeding at the pores, with dissolution. The scarlet stains upon the body and especially upon the face of the victim were the stigmas which shut him out from the aid and from the sympathy of his fellow men. And the whole seizure, progress, and termination of the disease, were the incidents of half an hour.

But the Prince Prospero was happy and dauntless and sagacious. When his dominions were half depopulated, he summoned a thousand hale and light-hearted friends from among the knights and dames of his court, and with these retired to the deep seclusion of one of his castellated abbeys. This was an extensive and magnificent structure, the creation of the prince's own eccentric yet august taste. A strong and lofty wall girdled it in. This wall had gates of iron. The courtiers, having entered, brought furnaces and massy hammers, and welded the bolts.

The abbey was amply provisioned. With such precautions the courtiers might bid defiance to contagion. The external world could take care of itself. In the meantime it was folly to grieve, or to think. The prince had provided all the appliances of pleasure. There were buffoons, there were ballet dancers, there were musicians, there was Beauty, there was wine. All these and security were within. Without was the "Red Death."

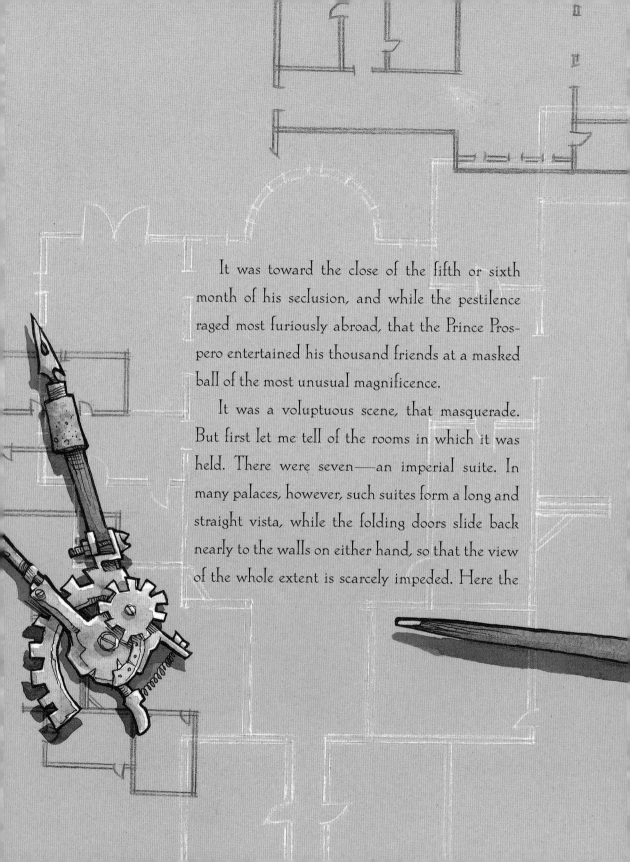

It was toward the close of the fifth or sixth month of his seclusion, and while the pestilence raged most furiously abroad, that the Prince Prospero entertained his thousand friends at a masked ball of the most unusual magnificence.

It was a voluptuous scene, that masquerade. But first let me tell of the rooms in which it was held. There were seven—an imperial suite. In many palaces, however, such suites form a long and straight vista, while the folding doors slide back nearly to the walls on either hand, so that the view of the whole extent is scarcely impeded. Here the

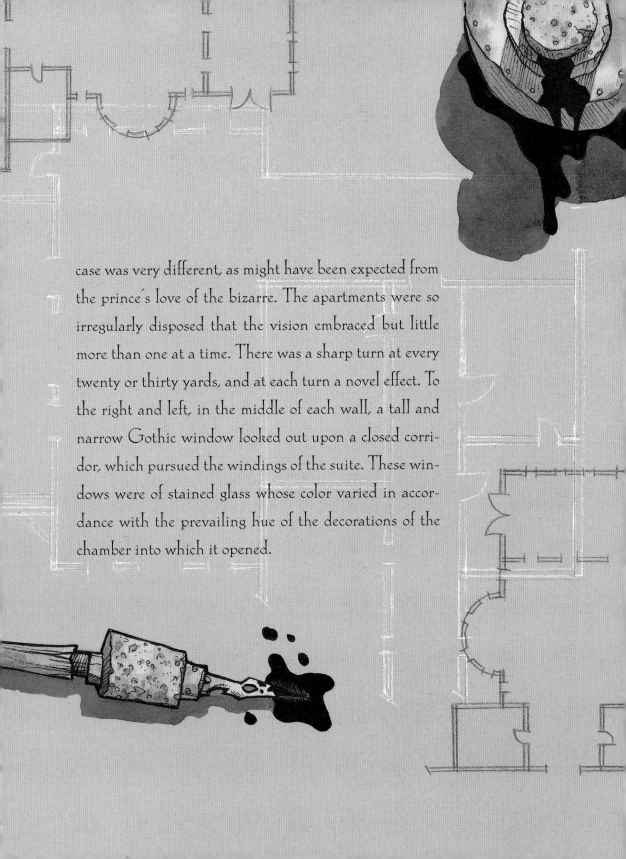

case was very different, as might have been expected from the prince's love of the bizarre. The apartments were so irregularly disposed that the vision embraced but little more than one at a time. There was a sharp turn at every twenty or thirty yards, and at each turn a novel effect. To the right and left, in the middle of each wall, a tall and narrow Gothic window looked out upon a closed corridor, which pursued the windings of the suite. These windows were of stained glass whose color varied in accordance with the prevailing hue of the decorations of the chamber into which it opened.

The chamber at the eastern extremity was hung in blue—and vividly blue were its windows.

The second chamber was purple in its ornaments and tapestries, and here the panes were purple.

The third was green throughout.

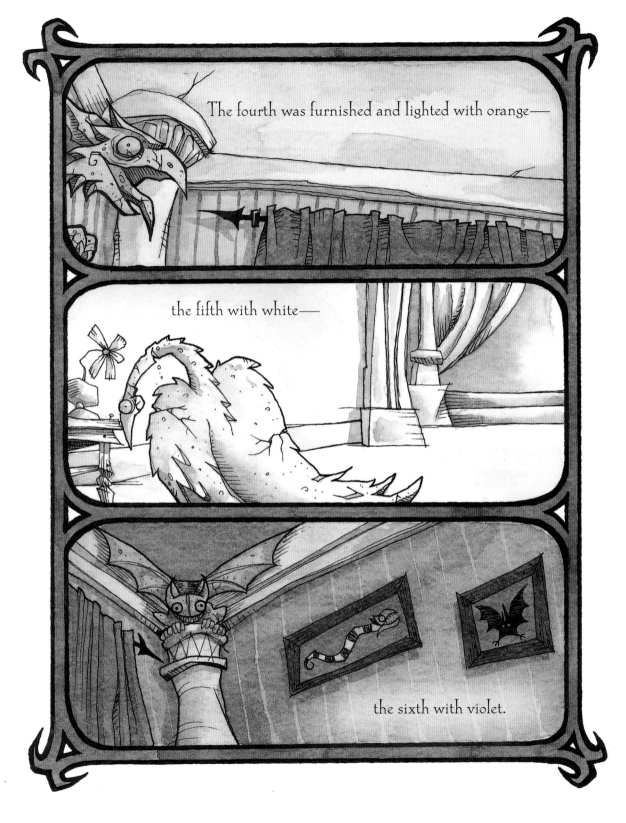

The fourth was furnished and lighted with orange—

the fifth with white—

the sixth with violet.

The seventh apartment was closely shrouded in black velvet tapestries that hung all over the ceiling and down the walls. But in this chamber only, the color of the windows failed to correspond with the decorations. The panes here were scarlet—a deep blood color.

Now in not one of the seven apartments was there any lamp or candelabrum, but in the corridors that followed the suite, there stood, opposite to each window, a heavy tripod, bearing a brazier of fire that projected its rays through the tinted glass and so glaringly illumined the room. But in the western or black chamber the effect of the fire-light that streamed upon the dark hangings through the blood-tinted panes, was ghastly in the extreme,

fig. 1

and produced so wild a look
upon the countenances of those
who entered, that there were few
of the company bold enough to set
foot within its precincts at all.

In this apartment stood a gigantic clock of ebony. Its pendulum
swung to and fro with a dull,
heavy, monotonous clang;

and when the minute-hand made the circuit of
the face, and the hour was to be stricken, there
came from the brazen lungs of the clock a sound
of so peculiar a note and emphasis that, at each
lapse of an hour, the musicians of the orchestra
were constrained to pause, momentarily, in
their performance,

and thus the waltzers ceased their revolutions;
and there was a brief disconcert of the whole gay
company; and the giddiest grew pale.

But when the echoes had fully ceased, a
light laughter at once pervaded the assembly;
the musicians looked at each other and smiled as
if at their own nervousness, and made whispering vows, each to
the other, that the next chiming of the clock should produce in
them no similar emotion; and then, after the lapse of sixty minutes,
there came yet another chiming of the clock, and then were the
same disconcert and tremulousness and meditation as before.

But, in spite of these things, it was a gay and magnificent revel. The tastes of the prince were peculiar. He had a fine eye for colors and effects. His plans were bold and fiery, and his conceptions glowed with barbaric luster.

He had directed, in great part, the movable embellishments of the seven chambers, upon occasion of this great fête; and it was his own guiding taste which had given character to the masqueraders. Be sure they were grotesque. There was much glare and glitter and piquancy and phantasm. There were delirious fancies such as the madman fashions. There was much of the beautiful, much of the wanton, much of the bizarre, something of the terrible, and not a little of that which might have excited disgust.

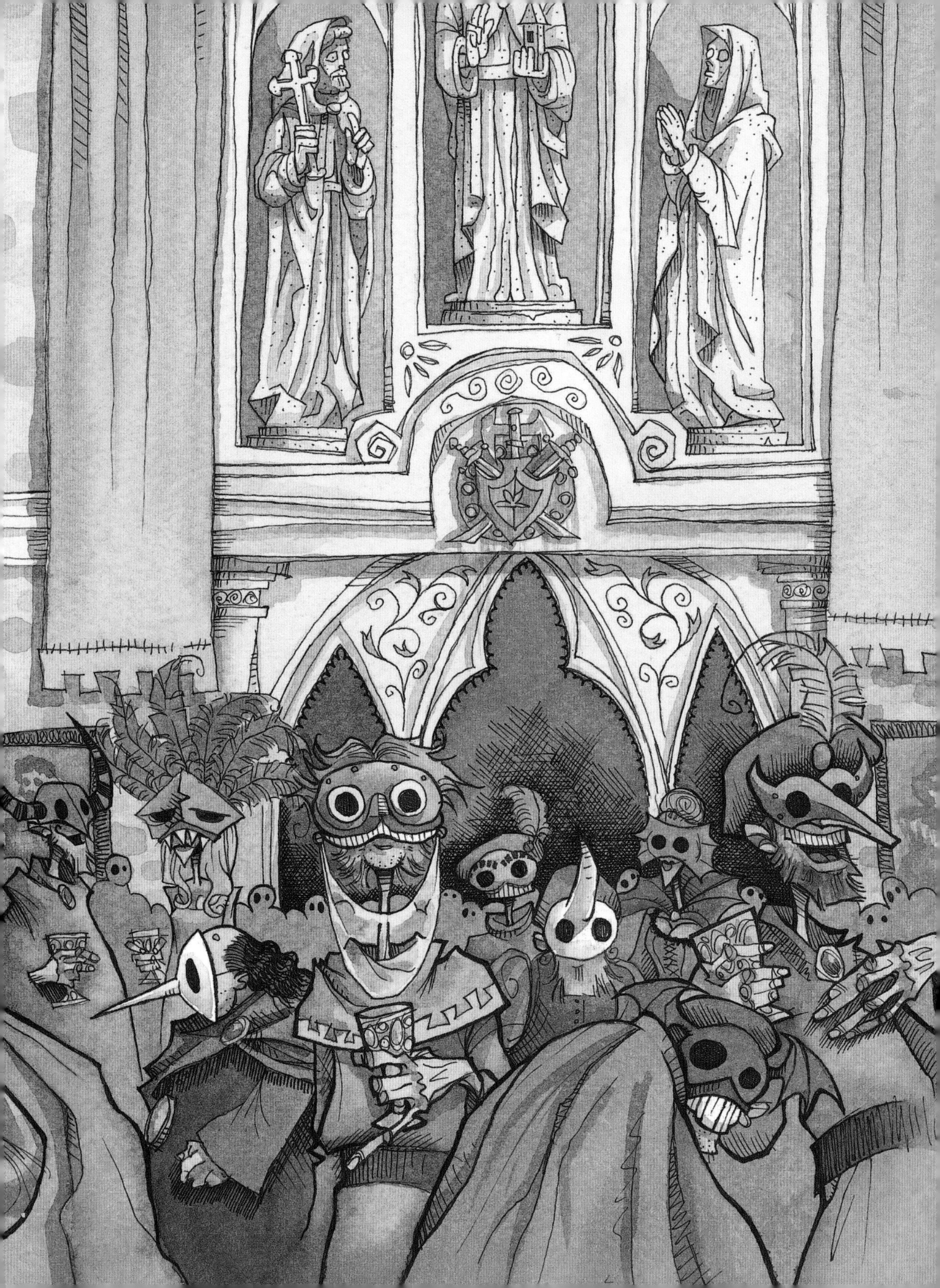

To the chamber which lies most westwardly of the seven, there are now none of the maskers who venture; for the night is waning away, and there flows a ruddier light through the blood-colored panes; and the blackness of the sable drapery appalls; and to him whose foot falls upon the sable carpet, there comes from the near clock of ebony a muffled peal more solemnly emphatic than any which reaches their ears who indulge in the more remote gaieties of the other apartments.

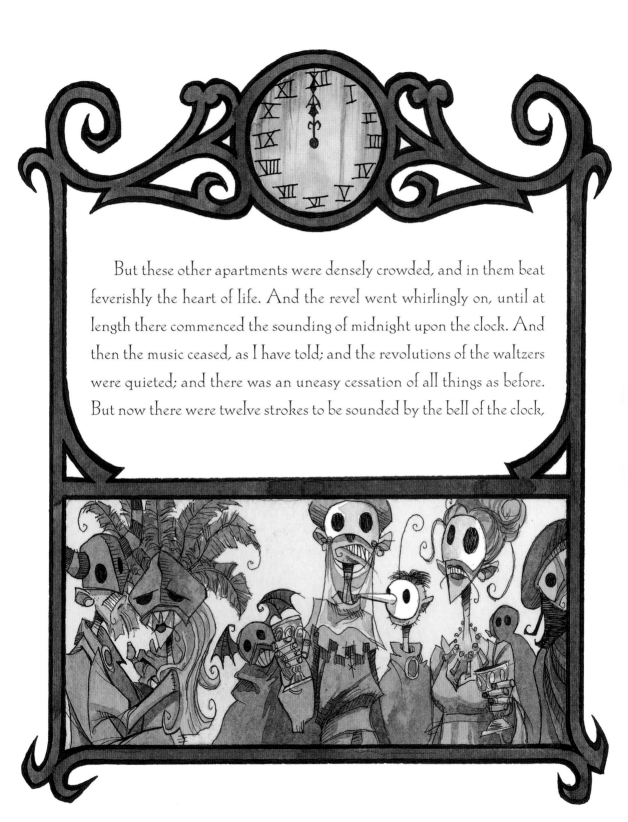

But these other apartments were densely crowded, and in them beat feverishly the heart of life. And the revel went whirlingly on, until at length there commenced the sounding of midnight upon the clock. And then the music ceased, as I have told; and the revolutions of the waltzers were quieted; and there was an uneasy cessation of all things as before. But now there were twelve strokes to be sounded by the bell of the clock,

and before the last echoes of the last chime had utterly sunk into silence, there were many individuals in the crowd who had found leisure to become aware of the presence of a masked figure which had arrested the attention of no single individual before.

And the rumor of this new presence having spread itself whisperingly around, there arose at length from the whole company a murmur, expressive of surprise—then, finally, of terror, of horror, and of disgust.

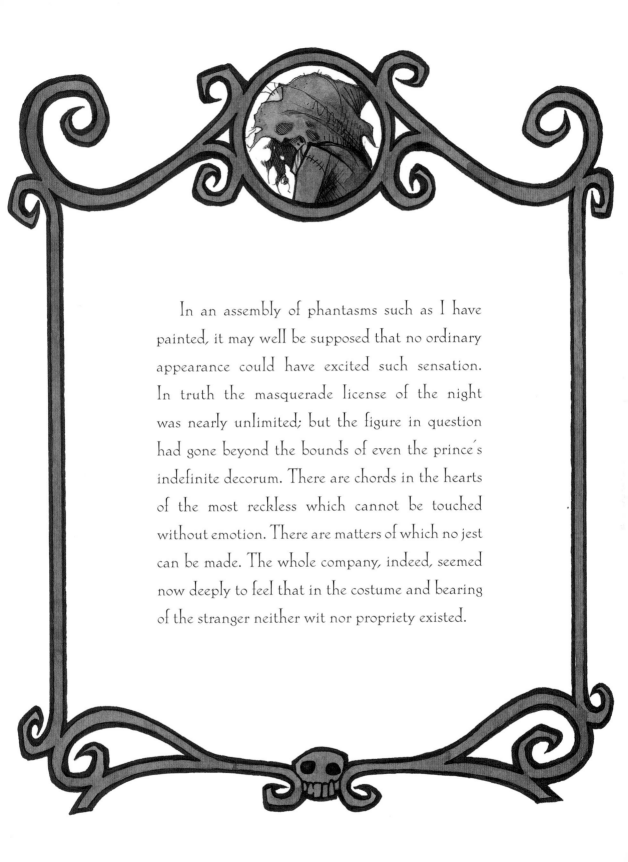

In an assembly of phantasms such as I have painted, it may well be supposed that no ordinary appearance could have excited such sensation. In truth the masquerade license of the night was nearly unlimited; but the figure in question had gone beyond the bounds of even the prince's indefinite decorum. There are chords in the hearts of the most reckless which cannot be touched without emotion. There are matters of which no jest can be made. The whole company, indeed, seemed now deeply to feel that in the costume and bearing of the stranger neither wit nor propriety existed.

The figure was tall and gaunt, and shrouded from head to foot in the habiliments of the grave. The mask which concealed the visage was made so nearly to resemble the countenance of a stiffened corpse that the closest scrutiny must have had difficulty in detecting the cheat. And yet all this might have been endured, if not approved, by the mad revelers around. But the mummer had gone so far as to assume the type of the Red Death. His vesture was dabbled in blood—and his broad brow, with all the features of the face, was besprinkled with the scarlet horror.

When the eyes of
Prince Prospero fell
upon this spectral image, he was seen to
be convulsed, in the first moment with a
strong shudder either of terror or distaste;

but, in the next, his brow reddened with rage.

"Who dares?"

he demanded hoarsely of the courtiers
who stood near him—

"Who dares insult us with this
blasphemous mockery? Seize him
and unmask him—that we may know
whom we have to hang, at sunrise
from the battlements!"

It was in the eastern or blue chamber in which stood the Prince Prospero as he uttered these words. They rang throughout the seven rooms loudly and clearly—for the prince was a bold and robust man, and the music had become hushed at the waving of his hand.

It was in the blue room where stood the prince, with a group of pale courtiers by his side. At first, as he spoke, there was a slight rushing movement of this group in the direction of the intruder, who at the moment was also near at hand, and now, with deliberate and stately step, made closer approach to the speaker.

But from a certain nameless awe with which the mad assumptions of the mummer had inspired the whole party, there were

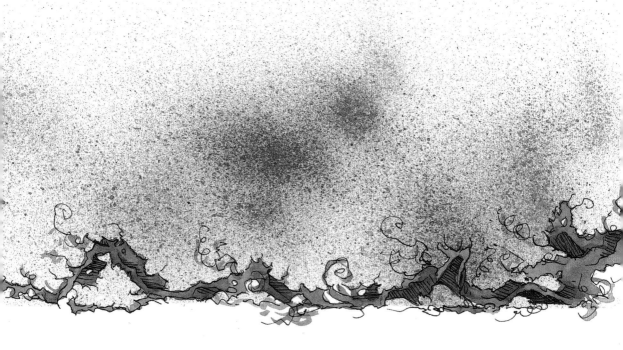

found none who put forth hand to seize him; so that, unimpeded, he passed within a yard of the prince's person; and, while the vast assembly, as if with one impulse, shrank from the centers of the rooms to the walls, he made his way uninterruptedly, but with the same solemn and measured step which had distinguished him from the first, through the blue chamber to the purple—through the purple to the green—through the green to the orange—through this again to the white— and even thence to the violet, before a decided movement had been made to arrest him.

It was then, however, that the Prince Prospero, maddening with rage and the shame of his own momentary cowardice, rushed hurriedly through the six chambers, while none followed him on account of a deadly terror that had seized upon all.

He bore aloft a drawn dagger, and had approached, in rapid impetuosity, to within three or four feet of the retreating figure,

when the latter, having attained the extremity of the velvet apartment, turned suddenly and confronted his pursuer.

There was a sharp cry—and the dagger dropped gleaming upon the sable carpet, upon which, instantly afterward, fell prostrate in death the Prince Prospero. Then, summoning the wild courage of despair, a throng of the revelers at once threw themselves into the black apartment, and, seizing the mummer, whose tall figure stood erect and motionless within the shadow of the ebony clock, gasped in unutterable horror at finding the grave-cerements and corpselike mask which they handled with so violent a rudeness, untenanted by any tangible form.

And now was acknowledged the presence of the Red Death. He had come like a thief in the night. And one by one dropped the revelers in the blood-bedewed halls of their revel, and died each in the despairing posture of his fall. And the life of the ebony clock went out with that of the last of the gay.

And the flames of the tripods expired. And Darkness and Decay and the Red Death held illimitable dominion over all.

Hop-Frog

I never knew anyone so keenly alive to a joke as the king was. He seemed to live only for joking. To tell a good story of the joke kind, and to tell it well, was the surest road to his favor. Thus it happened that his seven ministers were all noted for their accomplishments as jokers. They all took after the king, too, in being large, corpulent, oily men, as well as inimitable jokers. Whether people grow fat by joking, or whether there is something in fat itself which predisposes to a joke, I have never been quite able to determine; but certain it is that a lean joker is a *rara avis in terris*.

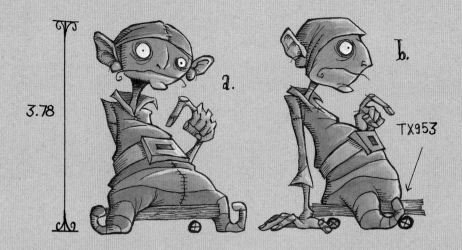

3.78

a.

b.

TX953

At the date of my narrative, professing jesters had not altogether gone out of fashion at court. Several of the great continental "powers" still retained their "fools," who wore motley, with caps and bells, and who were expected to be always ready with sharp witticisms.

Our king, as a matter of course, retained his "fool." The fact is, he *required* something in the way of folly——if only to counterbalance the heavy wisdom of the seven wise men who were his ministers——not to mention himself.

His fool, or professional jester, was not *only* a fool, however. His value was trebled in the eyes of the king, by the fact of his being also a dwarf and a cripple. Dwarfs were as common at court, in those days, as fools; and many monarchs would have found it difficult to get through their days (days are rather long at court than elsewhere) without both a jester to laugh with, and a dwarf to laugh at. But, as I have already observed, your jesters, in ninety-nine cases out of a hundred, are fat, round and unwieldy——so that it was no small source of self-gratulation with our king that, in Hop-Frog (this was the fool's name), he possessed a triplicate treasure in one person.

I believe the name "Hop-Frog" was not that given to the dwarf by his sponsors at baptism, but it was conferred upon him, by general consent of the seven ministers, on account of his inability to walk as other men do. In fact, Hop-Frog could only get along by a sort of interjectional gait—something between a leap and a wiggle—a movement that afforded illimitable amusement, and of course consolation, to the king, for (notwithstanding the protuberance of his stomach and a constitutional swelling of the head) the king, by his whole court, was accounted a capital figure.

But although Hop-Frog could move only with great pain and difficulty along a road or floor, the prodigious muscular power which nature seemed to have bestowed upon his arms enabled him to perform feats of wonderful dexterity, where trees or ropes were in question. At such exercises he certainly much more resembled a squirrel, or a small monkey, than a frog.

fig. 1

fig. 2

fig. 3

fig. 4

I am not able to say, with precision, from what country Hop-Frog originally came. It was from some barbarous region, however, that no person ever heard of— a vast distance from the court of our king. Hop-Frog and a young girl very little less dwarfish than himself (although of exquisite proportions, and a marvelous dancer) had been forcibly carried off from their respective homes in adjoining provinces and sent as presents to the king by one of his ever-victorious generals.

Under these circumstances, a close
intimacy arose between the two little captives.

Indeed, they soon became sworn friends. Hop-Frog,
although he made a great deal of sport, was by no means popular, had
it not in his power to render Trippetta many services; but *she*, on
account of her grace and exquisite beauty (although a dwarf), was
universally admired and petted; so she possessed much influence and
never failed to use it, whenever she could, for the benefit of Hop-Frog.

fig. 3

fig. 4

fig. 2

fig. 5

On some grand state occasion—I forgot what—the king determined to have a masquerade, and whenever a masquerade or anything of that kind occurred at our court, then the talents, both of Hop-Frog and Trippetta, were sure to be called into play. Hop-Frog was so inventive in the way of getting up pageants, suggesting novel characters, and arranging costumes for masked balls, that nothing could be done, it seems, without his assistance.

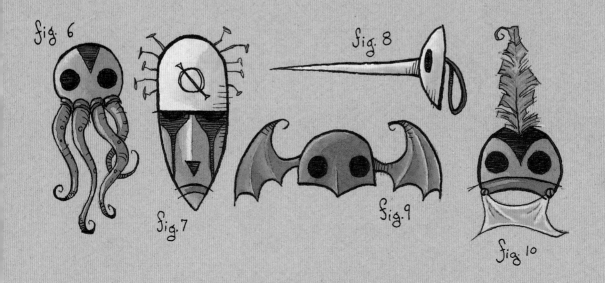

fig. 6

fig. 8

fig. 7

fig. 9

fig. 10

The night appointed for the fête had arrived. A gorgeous hall had been fitted up, under Trippetta's eye, with every kind of device which could possibly give éclat to a masquerade. The whole court was in a fever of expectation. As for costumes and characters, many had made up their minds (as to what roles they should assume) a week, or even a month, in advance; and, in fact, there was not a particle of indecision anywhere—except in the case of the king and his seven ministers. Why *they* hesitated I never could tell. At all events, time flew; and as a last resort they sent for Trippetta and Hop-Frog.

When the two little friends obeyed the summons of the king, they found him sitting at his wine with the seven members of his cabinet council. The monarch knew that Hop-Frog was not fond of wine, for it excited the poor cripple almost to madness.

But the king loved his practical jokes, and took pleasure in forcing Hop-Frog to drink and "to be merry."

"Come here, Hop-Frog,"

said he, as the jester and his friend entered the room:

"Swallow this bumper to the health of your absent friends

[here Hop-Frog sighed,]

"and then let us have the benefit of your invention. We want characters—*characters*, man—something novel. We are wearied with this everlasting sameness.

"Come, drink! The wine will brighten your wits."

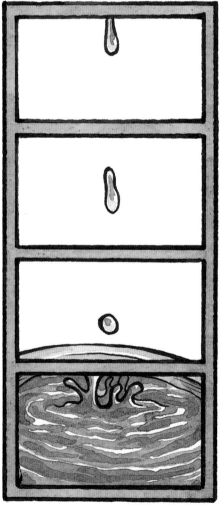

Hop-Frog endeavored, as usual, to get up a jest in reply to these advances from the king; but the effort was too much. It happened to be the poor dwarf's birthday, and the command to drink to his "absent friends" forced the tears to his eyes. Many large, bitter drops fell into the goblet as he took it, humbly, from the hand of the tyrant.

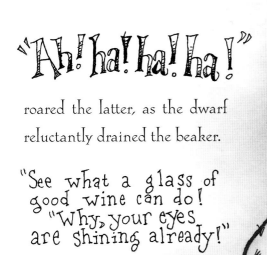

"Ah! ha! ha! ha!"

roared the latter, as the dwarf
reluctantly drained the beaker.

"See what a glass of
good wine can do!
"Why, your eyes
are shining already!"

Poor fellow! His large eyes *gleamed*, rather than shone; for
the effect of wine on his excitable brain was not more powerful
than instantaneous. He placed the goblet nervously on the table
and looked round upon the company with a half-insane stare.
They all seemed highly amused at the success of the king's *"joke."*

"And now to business," said the prime minister, a *very* fat man.

"Yes," said the king; "come, Hop-Frog, lend us your assistance. Characters, my fine fellow, we stand in need of characters—all of us—ha! ha! ha!"

Hee Hee Hee Hee

Hop-Frog also laughed, although feebly and somewhat vacantly.

"Come, come," said the king, impatiently, "have you nothing to suggest?"

"I am endeavoring to think of something *novel*," replied the dwarf, quite bewildered by the wine.

"Endeavoring!" cried the tyrant, fiercely;

"What do you mean by *that?* Ah, I perceive. You are sulky, and want more wine. Here, drink this!"

and he poured out another goblet full and offered it to the cripple, who merely gazed at it, gasping for breath.

"Drink, I say!" shouted the monster. "Or by the fiends—"

The dwarf hesitated. The king grew purple with rage. The courtiers smirked.

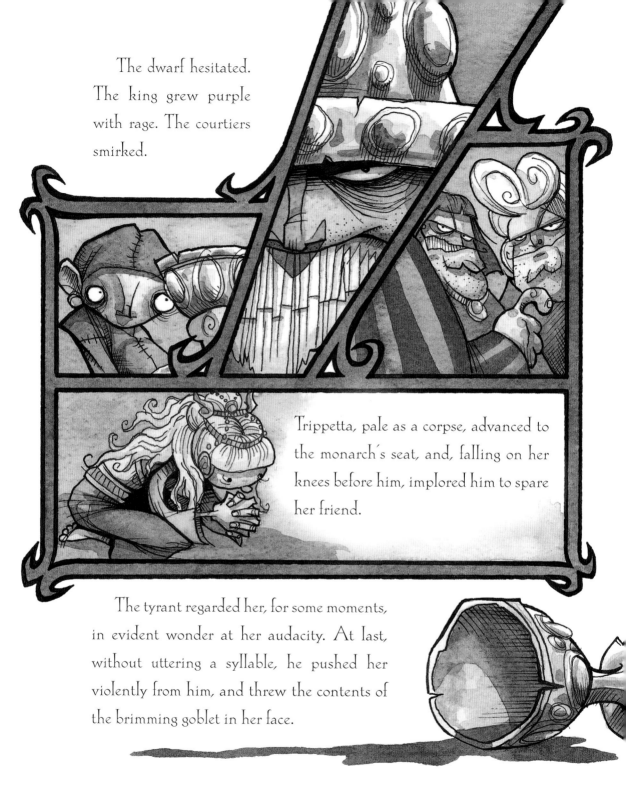

Trippetta, pale as a corpse, advanced to the monarch's seat, and, falling on her knees before him, implored him to spare her friend.

The tyrant regarded her, for some moments, in evident wonder at her audacity. At last, without uttering a syllable, he pushed her violently from him, and threw the contents of the brimming goblet in her face.

The poor girl got up the best she could and, not daring even to sigh, resumed her position at the foot of the table.

There was a dead silence for about half a minute. It was interrupted by a low but harsh and protracted *grating* sound which seemed to come at once from every corner of the room.

"What – what – *what are you making that noise for?*"

demanded the king, turning furiously to the dwarf.

The latter seemed to have recovered, in great measure, from his intoxication, and looking fixedly but quietly into the tyrant's face, merely responded:

"I – I? How could it have been me?"

"The sound appeared to come from without," observed one of the courtiers. "I fancy it was the parrot at the window whetting his bill upon his cage-wires."

"True," replied the monarch, as if much relieved by the suggestion; "but, on the honor of a knight, I could have sworn that it was the gritting of this vagabond's teeth."

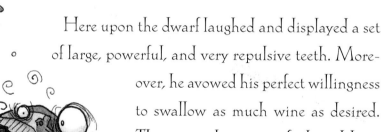

Here upon the dwarf laughed and displayed a set of large, powerful, and very repulsive teeth. Moreover, he avowed his perfect willingness to swallow as much wine as desired. The monarch was pacified; and having drained another bumper with no very perceptible ill effect, Hop-Frog entered at once, and with spirit, into the plans for the masquerade.

"I cannot tell what was the association of the idea," observed he, very tranquilly,

"but *just after* your majesty had done this, and while the parrot was making that odd noise outside the window, there came into my mind a capital diversion— one of my own country frolics—often enacted among us, at our masquerades; but here it will be new altogether. Unfortunately, however, it requires a company of eight persons, and—"

"Here we are!" cried the king, laughing at his acute discovery of the coincidence;

"eight to a fraction—I and my seven ministers. Come! What is the diversion?"

"We call it," replied the cripple,

"the Eight Chained Ourang-Outangs, and it really is excellent sport if well enacted."

"We will enact it," remarked the king, drawing himself up, and lowering his eyelids.

"The beauty of the game," continued Hop-Frog, "lies in the fright it occasions among the women."

"CAPITAL!" roared the monarch and his ministry.

"I will equip you as ourang-outangs," proceeded the dwarf; "leave all that to me. The resemblance shall be so striking, that the company of masqueraders will take you for real beasts — and, of course, they will be as much terrified as astonished."

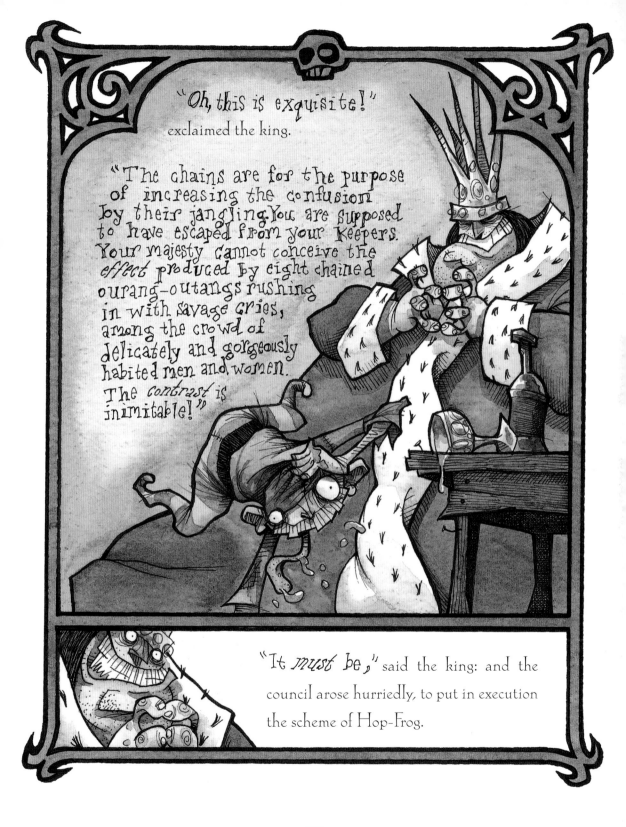

"Oh, this is exquisite!" exclaimed the king.

"The chains are for the purpose of increasing the confusion by their jangling. You are supposed to have escaped from your keepers. Your majesty cannot conceive the *effect* produced by eight chained ourang-outangs rushing in with savage cries, among the crowd of delicately and gorgeously habited men and women. The *contrast* is inimitable!"

"It *must be*," said the king: and the council arose hurriedly, to put in execution the scheme of Hop-Frog.

His mode of equipping the party as ourang-outangs was very simple. The animals in question had very rarely been seen in any part of the civilized world; and as the imitations made by the dwarf were sufficiently beastlike and more than sufficiently hideous, their truthfulness to nature was thus thought to be secured.

The king and his ministers were first encased in tight-fitting stockinet shirts and drawers, then saturated with tar. At this stage of the process, some one of the party suggested feathers, but the suggestion was at once overruled by the dwarf, who soon convinced the eight, by ocular demonstration, that the hair of such a brute as the ourang-outang was efficiently represented by *flax*. A thick coating of the latter was accordingly plastered upon the coating of tar. A long chain was now procured. First, it was passed about the waist of the king, *and tied*, then about another of the party, and also tied; then about all successively, in the same manner. When this chaining arrangement was complete, they formed a circle.

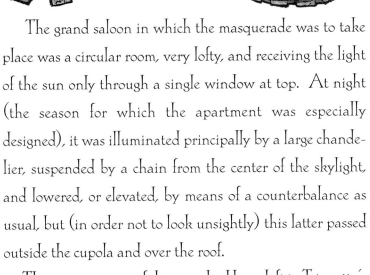

The grand saloon in which the masquerade was to take place was a circular room, very lofty, and receiving the light of the sun only through a single window at top. At night (the season for which the apartment was especially designed), it was illuminated principally by a large chandelier, suspended by a chain from the center of the skylight, and lowered, or elevated, by means of a counterbalance as usual, but (in order not to look unsightly) this latter passed outside the cupola and over the roof.

The arrangements of the room had been left to Trippetta's superintendence, but, in some particulars, it seems, she had been guided by the calmer judgment of her friend the dwarf. At his suggestion it was that, on this occasion, the chandelier was removed. Its waxen drippings (which, in weather so warm, it was quite impossible to prevent), would have been seriously detrimental to the rich dresses of the guests, who, on account of the crowded state of the saloon, could not all be expected to keep from out of its center—that is to say, from under the chandelier. Additional sconces were set in various parts of the hall, and a flambeau, emitting sweet odor, was placed in the right hand of each of the caryatides that stood against the wall—some fifty or sixty altogether.

The eight ourang-outangs, taking Hop-Frog's advice, waited patiently until midnight (when the room was thoroughly filled with masqueraders) before making their appearance. No sooner had the clock ceased striking, however, than they rushed, or rather rolled in, all together—for the impediments of their chains caused most of the party to fall, and all to stumble as they entered.

The excitement among the masqueraders was prodigious and filled the heart of the king with glee. As had been anticipated, there were not a few of the guests who supposed the ferocious-looking creatures to be beasts of *some* kind in reality, if not precisely ourang-outangs. Many of the women swooned with affright; and had not the king taken the precaution to exclude all weapons from the saloon, his party might soon have expiated their frolic in their blood. As it was, a general rush was made for the doors; but the king had ordered them to be locked immediately upon his entrance; and, at the dwarf's suggestion, the keys had been deposited with *him.*

While the tumult was at its height, and each masquerader attentive only to his own safety—the chain by which the chandelier ordinarily hung, and which had been drawn up on its removal, very gradually descended, until its hooked extremity came within three feet of the floor.

Soon after this, the king and his seven friends found themselves in the hall's center and in immediate contact with the chain. While they were thus situated, the dwarf, who had followed closely at their heels, inciting them to keep up the commotion, took hold of their chain and inserted the hook from which the chandelier had been wont to depend. In an instant, by some unseen agency, the chandelier-chain was drawn so far upward as to take the hook out of reach and drag the ourang-outangs together.

The masqueraders, by this time, had recovered from their alarm; and, beginning to regard the whole matter as a well-contrived pleasantry, set up a loud shout of laughter at the predicament of the apes.

"Leave them to *me*!"

now screamed Hop-Frog, his shrill voice making itself easily heard through all the din.

"Leave them to *me*. I fancy I know them. If I can only get a good look at them, I can soon tell who they are."

Here, scrambling over the heads of the crowd, he managed to get to the wall. Seizing a flambeau from one of the caryatides, he returned to the center of the room—

leaped with the agility of a monkey upon the king's head—

and thence clambered a few feet up the chain— holding down the torch to examine the group of ourang-outangs, and still screaming,

"I shall soon find out who they are!"

And now, while the whole assembly (the apes included) were convulsed with laughter, the jester suddenly uttered a shrill whistle. The chain flew violently up for about thirty feet— dragging with it the dismayed and struggling ourang-outangs, and leaving them suspended in mid-air between the skylight and the floor. Hop-Frog, clinging to the chain as it rose, still maintained his relative position in respect to the eight maskers, and still (as if nothing were the matter) continued to thrust his torch down toward them, as though endeavoring to discover who they were.

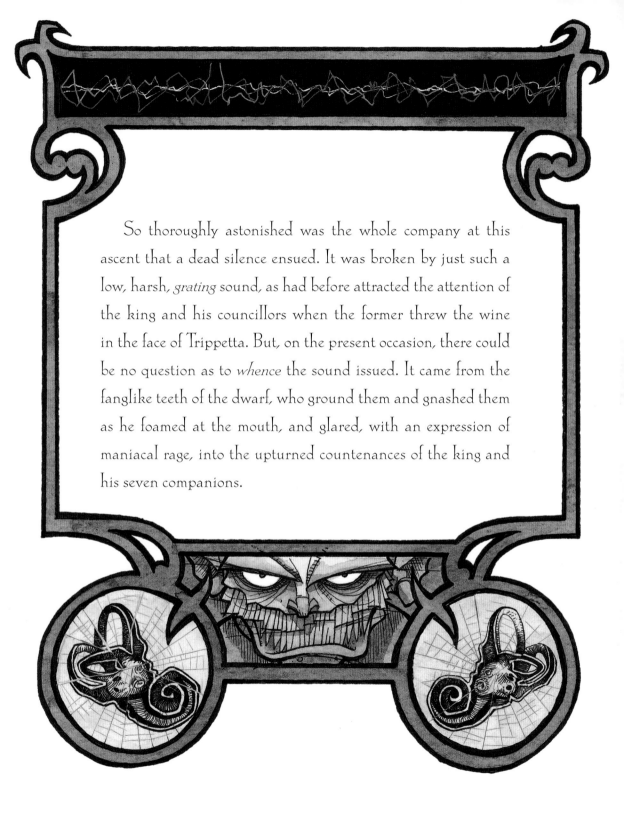

So thoroughly astonished was the whole company at this ascent that a dead silence ensued. It was broken by just such a low, harsh, *grating* sound, as had before attracted the attention of the king and his councillors when the former threw the wine in the face of Trippetta. But, on the present occasion, there could be no question as to *whence* the sound issued. It came from the fanglike teeth of the dwarf, who ground them and gnashed them as he foamed at the mouth, and glared, with an expression of maniacal rage, into the upturned countenances of the king and his seven companions.

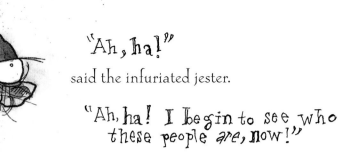

"Ah, ha!"

said the infuriated jester.

"Ah, ha! I begin to see who these people *are*, now!"

Here, pretending to scrutinize the king more closely, he held the flambeau to the flaxen coat which enveloped him and which instantly burst into a sheet of vivid flame.

In less than half a minute the whole eight ourang-outangs were blazing fiercely, amid the shrieks of the multitude who gazed at them from below, horror-stricken, and without the power to render them the slightest assistance.

At length the flames forced the jester to climb higher up the chain.

The dwarf once more spoke:

"I now see *distinctly*," he said, "what manner of people these maskers are. They are a great King and his seven privy-councillors—a King who does not scruple to strike a defenseless girl and his seven councillors who abet him in the outrage. As for myself, I am simply Hop-Frog, the jester—and *this is my last jest*."

Owing to the high combustibility of both the flax and the tar to which it adhered, the dwarf had scarcely made an end of his brief speech before the work of vengeance was complete. The eight corpses swung in their chains, a fetid, blackened, hideous, and indistinguishable mass. The cripple hurled his torch at them, clambered to the ceiling, and disappeared through the skylight.

It is supposed that Trippetta, stationed on the roof of the saloon, had been the accomplice of her friend in his fiery revenge, and that, together, they effected their escape to their own country, for neither was seen again.

The Fall of the House of Usher

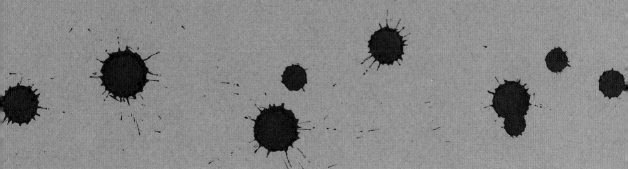

During the whole of a dull, dark, and soundless day in the autumn of the year, when the clouds hung oppressively low in the heavens,

I had been passing alone, on horse-back, through a singularly dreary tract of country,

and at length found myself, as the shades of the evening drew on, within view of the melancholy House of Usher.

I know not how it was, but, with the first glimpse of the building, a sense of insufferable gloom pervaded my spirit.

I looked upon the house and the simple landscape features of the domain—upon the bleak walls—upon the vacant eyelike windows—upon a few rank sedges—and upon a few white trunks of decayed trees—with an utter depression. There was an iciness, a sinking, a sickening of the heart. What was it—I paused to think—what was it that so unnerved me in the contemplation of the House of Usher? I was forced to fall back upon the unsatisfactory conclusion that while, beyond doubt, there are combinations of very simple natural objects which have the power of thus affecting us, still the reason, and the analysis, of this power lie among considerations beyond our depth.

It was possible, I reflected, that a mere different arrangement of the particulars of the scene, of the details of the picture, would be sufficient to modify, or perhaps to annihilate, its capacity for sorrowful impression; and, acting upon this idea,

I reined my horse to the precipitous brink of a black and lurid tarn that lay in unruffled luster by the dwelling, and gazed down—but with a shudder even more thrilling than before—upon the remodeled and inverted images of the gray sedge, and the ghastly tree-stems, and the vacant and eyelike windows.

Nevertheless, in this mansion of gloom I now proposed to myself a sojourn of some weeks. Its proprietor, Roderick Usher, had been one of my boon companions in boyhood, but many years had elapsed since our last meeting.

A letter, however, had lately reached me—a letter from him—which, in its wildly importunate nature, had admitted of no other than a personal reply. The writer spoke of acute bodily illness—of a pitiable mental idiosyncrasy which oppressed him—and of an earnest desire to see me, as his best, and indeed, his only personal friend, with a view of attempting, by the cheerfulness of my society, some alleviation of his malady. It was the apparent *heart* that went with his request—which allowed me no room for hesitation.

Although, as boys, we had been even intimate associates, I really knew little of my friend. I had learned the very remarkable fact that the stem of the Usher race, all time-honored as it was, had put forth, at no period, any enduring branch; in other words, that the entire family lay in the direct line of descent, and had always, with very trifling and very temporary variation, so lain. It was this deficiency and the consequent undeviating transmission, from sire to son, of the patrimony with the name, which had, at length, so identified the two as to merge the original title of the estate in the quaint and equivocal appellation of the "House of Usher"—an appellation which seemed to include both the family and the family mansion.

The
HOUSE
of
USHER

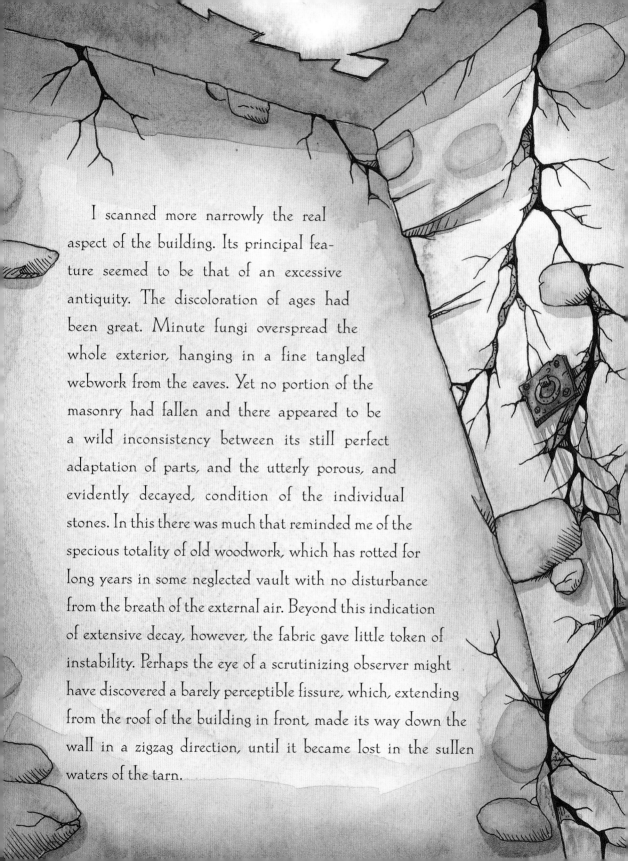

I scanned more narrowly the real aspect of the building. Its principal feature seemed to be that of an excessive antiquity. The discoloration of ages had been great. Minute fungi overspread the whole exterior, hanging in a fine tangled webwork from the eaves. Yet no portion of the masonry had fallen and there appeared to be a wild inconsistency between its still perfect adaptation of parts, and the utterly porous, and evidently decayed, condition of the individual stones. In this there was much that reminded me of the specious totality of old woodwork, which has rotted for long years in some neglected vault with no disturbance from the breath of the external air. Beyond this indication of extensive decay, however, the fabric gave little token of instability. Perhaps the eye of a scrutinizing observer might have discovered a barely perceptible fissure, which, extending from the roof of the building in front, made its way down the wall in a zigzag direction, until it became lost in the sullen waters of the tarn.

Noticing these things, I rode over a short causeway to the house.

A servant in waiting took my horse, and I entered the Gothic archway of the hall.

A valet thence conducted me, in silence, through many dark and intricate passages to the studio of his master.

Much that I encountered on the way contributed to heightening the vague sentiments of which I have already spoken. While the objects around me—the carvings of the ceilings, the somber tapestries of the walls, the ebon blackness of the floors, and the phantasmagoric armorial trophies which rattled as I strode, were but matters to which, or to such as which, I had been accustomed from my infancy—I still wondered to find how unfamiliar were the fancies which ordinary images were stirring up.

On one of the staircases, I met the physician of the family. His countenance, I thought, wore a mingled expression of low cunning and perplexity. He accosted me with trepidation and passed on.

The valet now threw open a door and ushered me into the presence of his master.

The room in which I found myself was very large and excessively lofty. The windows were long, narrow, and pointed, and at so vast a distance from the black oaken floor as to be altogether inaccessible from within. Feeble gleams of encrimsoned light made their way through the trellised panes and served to render sufficiently distinct the more prominent objects around; the eye, however, struggled in vain to reach the remoter angles of the chamber, or the recesses of the vaulted and fretted ceiling.

Dark draperies hung upon the walls. The general furniture was profuse, comfortless, antique, and tattered. Many books and musical instruments lay scattered about, but failed to give any vitality to the scene. I felt that I breathed an atmosphere of sorrow.

Upon my entrance Usher arose from a sofa on which he had been lying, and greeted me with a vivacious warmth which had much in it, I at first thought, of an overdone cordiality. A glance, however, at his countenance convinced me of his perfect sincerity.

We sat down; and for some moments, while he spoke not, I gazed upon him with a feeling half of pity, half of awe.

Surely, man had never before so terribly altered, in so brief a period, as had

Roderick Usher!

Yet the character of his face had been at all times remarkable. A cadaverousness of complexion; an eye large, liquid, and luminous beyond comparison; lips somewhat thin and very pallid, but of a surpassingly beautiful curve; a nose of a delicate Hebrew model; a finely molded chin, speaking, in its want of prominence, of a want of moral energy; hair of a more than weblike softness; these features made up altogether a countenance not easily to be forgotten. And now in the mere exaggeration of the prevailing character of these features, lay so much of change that I doubted to whom I spoke. The now ghastly pallor of the skin, and the now miraculous luster of the eye, above all things startled and even awed me. The silken hair, too, had been suffered to grow all unheeded, and in its wild gossamer texture, it floated rather than fell about the face.

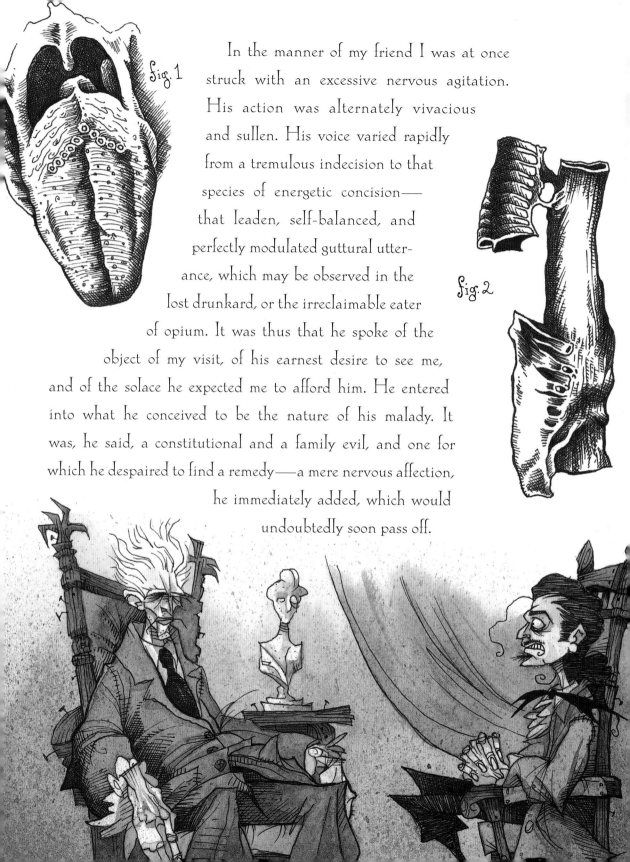

fig. 1

fig. 2

In the manner of my friend I was at once struck with an excessive nervous agitation. His action was alternately vivacious and sullen. His voice varied rapidly from a tremulous indecision to that species of energetic concision— that leaden, self-balanced, and perfectly modulated guttural utterance, which may be observed in the lost drunkard, or the irreclaimable eater of opium. It was thus that he spoke of the object of my visit, of his earnest desire to see me, and of the solace he expected me to afford him. He entered into what he conceived to be the nature of his malady. It was, he said, a constitutional and a family evil, and one for which he despaired to find a remedy—a mere nervous affection, he immediately added, which would undoubtedly soon pass off.

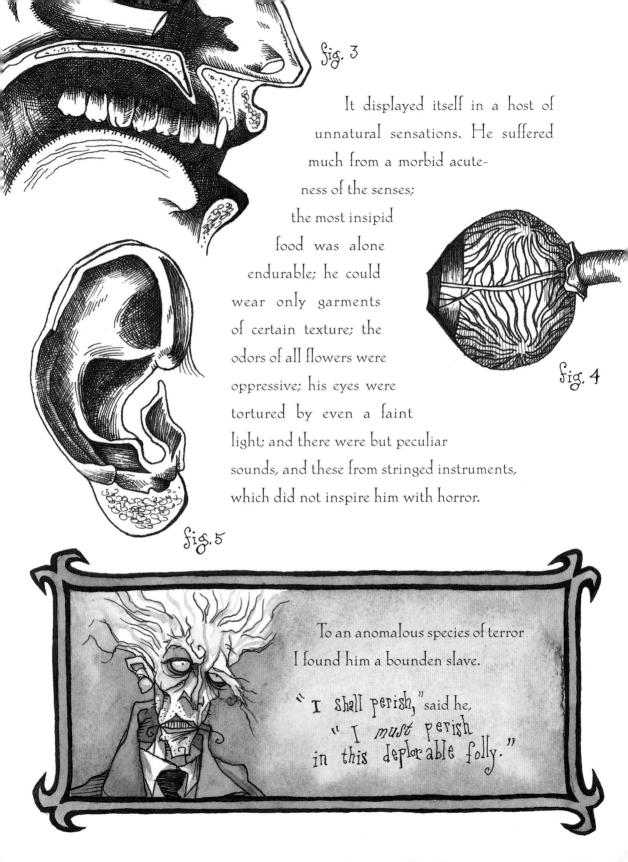

fig. 3

fig. 4

fig. 5

It displayed itself in a host of unnatural sensations. He suffered much from a morbid acuteness of the senses; the most insipid food was alone endurable; he could wear only garments of certain texture; the odors of all flowers were oppressive; his eyes were tortured by even a faint light; and there were but peculiar sounds, and these from stringed instruments, which did not inspire him with horror.

To an anomalous species of terror I found him a bounden slave.

"I shall perish," said he, "I must perish in this deplorable folly."

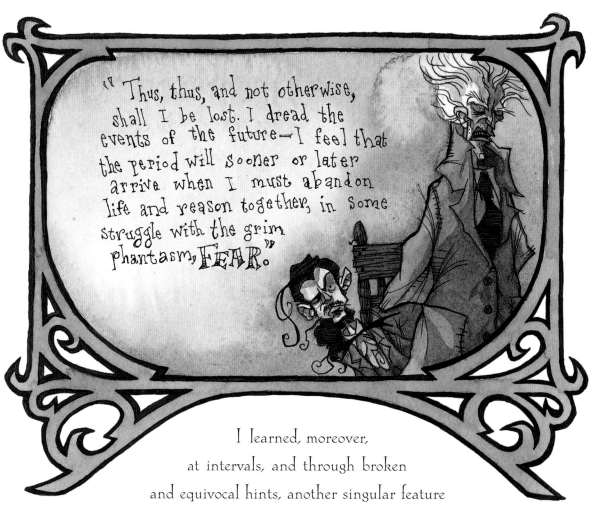

"Thus, thus, and not otherwise, shall I be lost. I dread the events of the future—I feel that the period will sooner or later arrive when I must abandon life and reason together, in some struggle with the grim phantasm, FEAR."

I learned, moreover, at intervals, and through broken and equivocal hints, another singular feature of his mental condition. He was enchained by certain superstitious impressions in regard to the dwelling which he tenanted, and whence, for many years, he had never ventured forth—in regard to an influence whose force was conveyed in terms too shadowy here to be restated—an influence which some peculiarities in the mere form and substance of his family mansion had, by dint of long sufferance, he said, obtained over his spirit—an effect which the physique of the gray walls and turrets, and of the dim tarn into which they all looked down, had, at length, brought about upon the morale of his existence.

He admitted, however, that much of the peculiar gloom which thus afflicted him could be traced to the severe and long-continued illness—indeed to the evidently approaching dissolution—of a tenderly beloved sister, his sole companion for long years—his last and only relative on Earth. "Her decease," he said, with a bitterness which I can never forget, "would leave me the last of the ancient race of the Ushers."

While he spoke, the lady Madeline (for so was she called) passed slowly through a remote portion of the apartment, and, without having noticed my presence, disappeared.

I regarded her with an utter astonishment not unmingled with dread—and yet I found it impossible to account for such feelings. A sensation of stupor oppressed me, as my eyes followed her retreating steps.

The disease of the lady Madeline had long baffled the skill of her physicians. A settled apathy and a gradual wasting away of the person were the unusual diagnoses. Hitherto she had steadily borne up against the pressure of her malady, and had not betaken herself finally to bed; but, on the closing in of the evening of my arrival at the house, she succumbed to the prostrating power of the destroyer; and I learned that the glimpse I had obtained of her person would thus probably be the last I should obtain—that the lady, at least while living, would be seen by me no more.

For several days ensuing, her name was unmentioned by either Usher or myself; and during this period, I was busied in earnest endeavors to alleviate the melancholy of my friend.

We painted and read together—or I listened, as if in a dream, to the wild improvisations of his speaking guitar.

And thus the more bitterly did I perceive the futility of all attempt at cheering a mind from which darkness poured forth upon all objects of the moral and physical universe, in one unceasing radiation of gloom.

I shall ever bear about me a memory of the many solemn hours I thus spent alone with the master of the House of Usher. An excited and highly distempered ideality threw a sulphurous luster over all. The paintings, over which his elaborate fancy brooded, grew, touch by touch, into vaguenesses at which I shuddered the more thrillingly. If ever a mortal painted an idea, that mortal was Roderick Usher. For me at least—in the circumstances then surrounding me—there arose out of the pure abstractions which the hypochondriac contrived to throw upon his canvas an intensity of intolerable awe.

One of the phantasmagoric conceptions of my friend may be shadowed forth, although feebly, in words. A small picture presented the interior of an immensely long and rectangular vault or tunnel, with low walls, smooth, white, and without interruption or device.

No outlet was observed in any portion of its vast extent, and no torch or other artificial source of light was discernible—yet a flood of intense rays rolled throughout and bathed the whole in a ghastly and inappropriate splendor.

I have just spoken of that morbid condition of the auditory nerve, which rendered all music intolerable to the sufferer, with the exception of certain effects of stringed instruments. It was, perhaps, the narrow limits to which he thus confined himself upon the guitar, which gave birth in great measure, to the fantastic character of his performances.

But the fervid facility of his impromptus could not be so accounted for.

They must have been, and were, the result of that intense mental collectedness and concentration to which I have previously alluded as observable only in particular moments of the highest artificial excitement. The words of one of these rhapsodies I have easily remembered. I fancied that I perceived, and for the first time, a full consciousness on the part of Usher, of the tottering of his lofty reason.

The last of the verses, which was entitled "The Haunted Palace," ran very nearly, if not accurately, thus:

I

In the greenest of our valleys,
By good angels tenanted,
Once a fair and stately palace—
Radiant palace—reared its head.
In the monarch Thought's dominion—
It stood there!
Never seraph spread a pinion
Over fabric half so fair.

II

Banners yellow, glorious, golden,
On its roof did float and flow;
(This—all this—was in the olden
Time long ago)
And every gentle air that dallied,
In that sweet day,
Along the ramparts plumed and pallid,
A winged odor went away.

III

Wanderers in that happy valley
Through two luminous windows saw
Spirits moving musically
To a lute's well-tuned law,
Round about a throne, where sitting
(Porphyrogene!)
In state his glory well befitting,
The ruler of the realm was seen.

IV

And all with pearl and ruby glowing
Was the fair palace door,
Through which came flowing, flowing, flowing,
And sparkling evermore,
A troop of Echoes whose sweet duty
Was but to sing,
In voices of surpassing beauty,
The wit and wisdom of their king.

V

But evil things, in robes of sorrow,
Assailed the monarch's high estate;
(Ah, let us mourn, for never morrow
Shall dawn upon him, desolate!)
And, round about his home, the glory
That blushed and bloomed
Is but a dim-remembered story
Of the old time entombed.

VI

And travelers now within that valley,
Through the red-litten windows, see
Vast forms that move fantastically
To a discordant melody;
While, like a rapid ghastly river,
Through the pale door,
A hideous throng rush out forever,
And laugh—but smile no more.

I well remember that suggestions arising from this ballad led us to an opinion of Usher's, of the sentience of all vegetable things. The belief was connected with the gray stones of the home of his forefathers. The conditions of the sentience had been here, he imagined, fulfilled in the method of collocation of these stones—in the order of their arrangement, as well as in that of the many fungi which overspread them, and of the decayed trees which stood around—above all, in the long undisturbed endurance of this arrangement, and in its reduplication in the still waters of the tarn. The evidence of the sentience was to be seen, he said, in the gradual yet certain condensation of an atmosphere of their own about the waters and the walls. The result was discoverable, he added, in that silent, yet importunate and terrible influence, which for centuries had molded the destinies of his family, and which made *him* what I now saw him—what he was.

One evening, having informed me abruptly that the lady Madeline was no more, he stated his intention of preserving her corpse for a fortnight, in one of the numerous vaults within the main walls of the building.

The worldly reason assigned for this singular proceeding was one which I did not feel at liberty to dispute. The brother had been led to his resolution by consideration of the unusual character of the malady of the deceased, of certain obtrusive and eager inquiries on the part of her medical men, and of the remote and exposed situation of the burial ground of the family. I will not deny that when I called to mind the sinister countenance of the person whom I met upon the staircase, on the day of my arrival at the house, I had no desire to oppose what I regarded as a harmless, and not by any means an unnatural, precaution.

At the request of Usher, I personally aided him in the arrangements for the temporary entombment. The body having been encoffined, we two alone bore it to its rest.

The vault in which we placed it was small, damp, and entirely without means of admission for light; lying, at great depth, immediately beneath that portion of the building in which was my own sleeping apartment.

A portion of its floor, and the whole interior of a long archway through which we reached it, were carefully sheathed with copper. The door, of massive iron, had been, also, similarly protected. Its immense weight caused an unusually sharp grating sound, as it moved upon its hinges.

Having deposited our mournful burden, we partially turned aside the yet unscrewed lid of the coffin, and looked upon the face of the tenant. A striking similitude between the brother and sister now arrested my attention; and Usher, divining, perhaps, my thoughts, murmured out some few words from which I learned that the deceased and himself had been twins, and that sympathies of a scarcely intelligible nature had always existed between them. Our glances, however, rested not long upon the dead—for we could not regard her unawed. The disease, which had thus entombed the lady in the maturity of youth, had left, as usual in all maladies of a strictly cataleptical character, the mockery of a faint blush upon the bosom and the face, and that suspiciously lingering smile upon the lip. We replaced and screwed down the lid, and, having secured the door of iron, made our way into the scarcely less gloomy apartments of the upper portion of the house.

And now, some days of bitter grief having elapsed, an observable change came over the features of the mental disorder of my friend. His ordinary manner had vanished. The pallor of his countenance had assumed, if possible, a more ghastly hue—but the luminousness of his eye had utterly gone out. There were times, indeed, when I thought his unceasingly agitated mind was laboring with an oppressive secret, to divulge which he struggled for the necessary courage. At times, I was obliged to resolve all into the mere inexplicable vagaries of madness, as I beheld him gazing upon vacancy for long hours, in an attitude of the profoundest attention, as if listening to some imaginary sound. It was no wonder that his condition terrified—that it infected me. I felt creeping upon me the wild influences of his own fantastic yet impressive superstitions.

It was upon retiring to bed late in the night of the seventh or eighth day after the placing of the lady Madeline within the vault, that I experienced the full power of such feelings. Sleep came not near my couch—while the hours waned away.

I struggled to reason off the nervousness which had dominion over me. An irrepressible tremor gradually pervaded my frame; and, at length, there sat upon my very heart an incubus of utterly causeless alarm.

Shaking this off with a gasp and a struggle, I uplifted myself upon the pillows and, peering earnestly within the intense darkness of the chamber, harkened to certain low and indefinite sounds, which came, through the pauses of the storm, at long intervals.

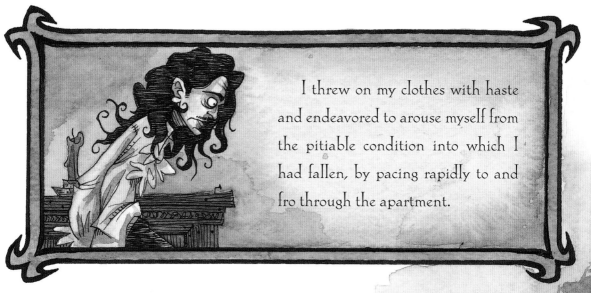

I threw on my clothes with haste and endeavored to arouse myself from the pitiable condition into which I had fallen, by pacing rapidly to and fro through the apartment.

I had taken but few turns in this manner, when a light step on an adjoining staircase arrested my attention. I presently recognized it as that of Usher. In an instant afterward he rapped, with a gentle touch, at my door, and entered. His countenance was, as usual, cadaverously wan—but there was a mad hilarity in his eyes—an evident restrained *hysteria* in his whole demeanor. His air appalled me—but anything was preferable to the solitude which I had so long endured, and I even welcomed his presence as a relief.

"And you have not seen it?" he said abruptly, after having stared about him for some moments in silence—

"You have not then seen it?— but, stay! You shall."

Thus speaking, he hurried to one of the gigantic casements and threw it freely open to the storm.

The impetuous fury of the entering gust nearly lifted us from our feet. It was, indeed, a tempestuous yet sternly beautiful night, and one wildly singular in its terror and its beauty.

A whirlwind had apparently
collected its force in our vicinity; for
there were frequent and violent alterations in
the direction of the wind; and the exceeding density
of the clouds did not prevent our perceiving the
lifelike velocity with which they flew careering from
all points against each other, without passing away
into the distance. The undersurfaces of the huge
masses of agitated vapor, as well as all terrestrial
objects immediately around us, were glowing in the
unnatural light of a faintly luminous and distinctly
visible gaseous exhalation which hung about
and enshrouded the mansion.

"You must not—
You shall not behold this!"
said I, shudderingly, to Usher,
as I led him to a seat.

"These appearances, which
bewilder you, are merely electrical
phenomena not uncommon—
or it may be that they have
their ghastly origin in the
rank miasma of the tarn.
Let us close this casement—
the air is chilling and
dangerous to your frame."

"Here is one of your
favorite romances. I will
read, and you shall
listen—and so we will
pass away this terrible
night together."

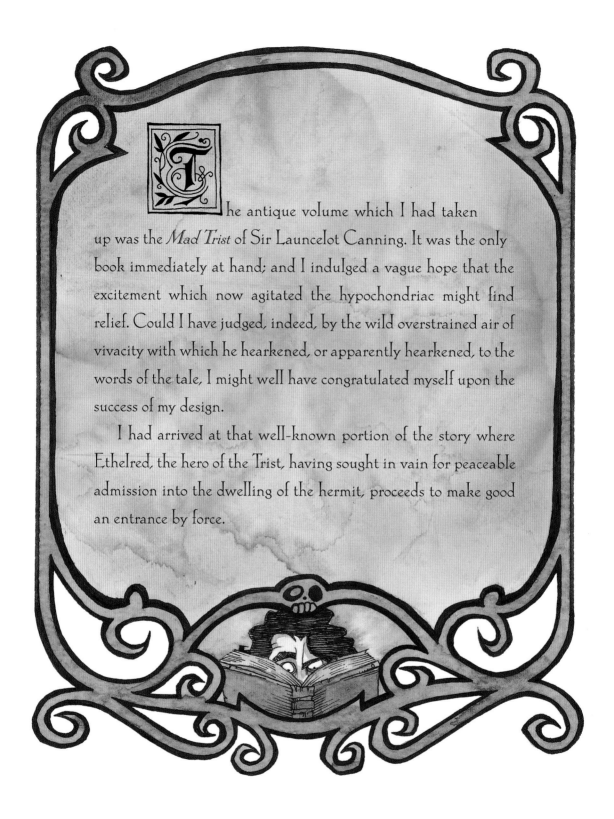

The antique volume which I had taken up was the *Mad Trist* of Sir Launcelot Canning. It was the only book immediately at hand; and I indulged a vague hope that the excitement which now agitated the hypochondriac might find relief. Could I have judged, indeed, by the wild overstrained air of vivacity with which he hearkened, or apparently hearkened, to the words of the tale, I might well have congratulated myself upon the success of my design.

I had arrived at that well-known portion of the story where Ethelred, the hero of the Trist, having sought in vain for peaceable admission into the dwelling of the hermit, proceeds to make good an entrance by force.

"Ethelred, with blows, made room in the plankings of the door for his gauntleted hand; and now cracked, and ripped, and tore all asunder, that the noise of the dry and hollow-sounding wood reverberated throughout the forest."

At the termination of this sentence I started, and for a moment, paused; for it appeared to me that, from some very remote portion of the mansion, there came, indistinctly, to my ears, what might have been, in its exact similarity of character, the echo of the very cracking and ripping sound which Sir Launcelot had so particularly described. It was, beyond doubt, the coincidence alone which had arrested my attention; for, amid the rattling of the sashes of the casements, and the ordinary commingled noises of the still-increasing storm, the sound, in itself, had nothing, surely, which should have interested or disturbed me.

I continued the story

"But the good champion Ethelred, now entering within the door, was sore enraged and amazed to perceive no signal of the maliceful hermit; but, in the stead thereof, a dragon of a scaly and prodigious demeanor, and of a fiery tongue.

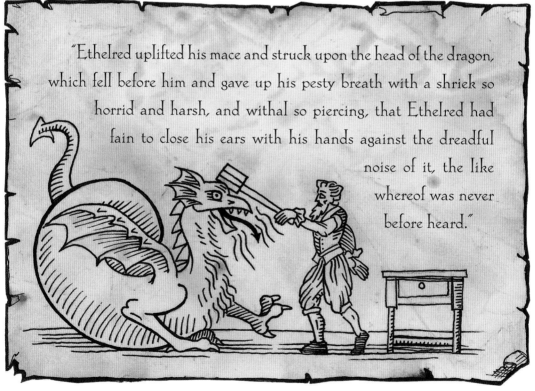

"Ethelred uplifted his mace and struck upon the head of the dragon, which fell before him and gave up his pesty breath with a shriek so horrid and harsh, and withal so piercing, that Ethelred had fain to close his ears with his hands against the dreadful noise of it, the like whereof was never before heard."

128

Here again I paused abruptly, and now with a feeling of wild amazement—for there could be no doubt whatever that I did actually hear a most unusual screaming sound.

I still retained sufficient presence of mind to avoid exciting the sensitive nervousness of my companion. I was by no means certain that he had noticed the sounds in question; although, assuredly, a strange alteration had taken place in his demeanor. From a position fronting my own, he had gradually brought round his chair, so as to sit with his face to the door of the chamber. I saw that his lips trembled as if he were murmuring inaudibly. His head had dropped upon his breast—yet I knew that he was not asleep, from the wide and rigid opening of the eye as I caught a glance of it in profile. The motion of his body, too, was at variance with this idea— for he rocked from side to side with a gentle yet constant and uniform sway. Having rapidly taken notice of all this,

I resumed the narrative of Sir Launcelot, which thus proceeded:

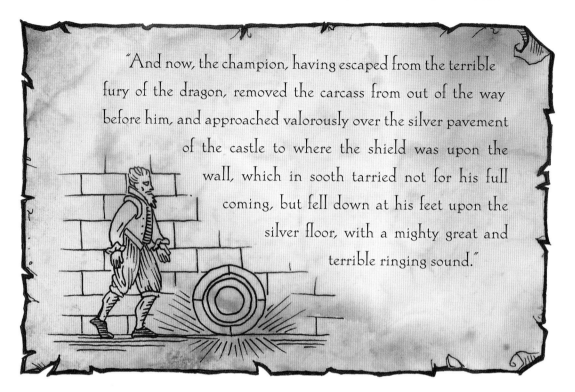

"And now, the champion, having escaped from the terrible fury of the dragon, removed the carcass from out of the way before him, and approached valorously over the silver pavement of the castle to where the shield was upon the wall, which in sooth tarried not for his full coming, but fell down at his feet upon the silver floor, with a mighty great and terrible ringing sound."

No sooner had these syllables passed my lips, than—as if a shield of brass had indeed, at the moment, fallen heavily upon a floor of silver—I became aware of a distinct, hollow, metallic, and clangorous, yet apparently muffled reverberation.

Completely unnerved, I leaped to my feet; but the measured rocking movement of Usher was undisturbed. As I placed my hand upon his shoulder, there came a strong shudder over his whole person; a sickly smile quivered about his lips; and I saw that he spoke in a low, hurried, and gibbering murmur, as if unconscious of my presence. Bending closely over him, I at length drank in the hideous import of his words.

"Not hear it?"

" – yes, I hear it, and *have* heard it. Long–long–long–many minutes, many hours, many days, have I heard it– yet I dared not–oh, pity me, miserable wretch that I am!–I dared not– I *dared* not SPEAK!"

"We have put her living in the tomb!"

"Said I not that my senses were acute? I *now* tell you that I heard her first feeble movements in the hollow coffin. I heard them—many, many days ago—yet I dared not—*I dared not speak!* And now—tonight—Ethelred—ha! ha!—the breaking of the hermit's door, and the death cry of the dragon, and the clangor of the shield!—say, rather, the rending of her coffin, and the grating of the iron hinges of her prison, and her struggles within the coppered archway of the vault! Oh whither shall I fly? Will she not be here anon? Is she not hurrying to upbraid me for my haste? Have I not heard her footstep on the stair? Do I not distinguish that heavy and horrible beating of her heart?

"MADMAN!"

—here he sprang furiously to his feet, and shrieked out his syllables—

"MADMAN! I TELL YOU THAT SHE NOW STANDS WITHOUT THE DOOR!"

As if in the superhuman energy of his utterance there had been found the potency of a spell—the huge antique panels to which the speaker pointed threw slowly back, upon the instant, their ponderous and ebony jaws. It was the work of the rushing gust—then there DID stand the lofty and enshrouded figure of the lady Madeline of Usher. There was blood upon her white robes, and the evidence of some bitter struggle upon every portion of her emaciated frame.

For a moment she remained trembling and reeling to and fro upon the threshold—then, with a low moaning cry, fell heavily inward upon the person of her brother, and in her violent death-agonies, bore him to the floor a corpse, and a victim to the terrors he had anticipated.

From that chamber, and from that mansion, I fled, aghast. The storm was still abroad in all its wrath as I found myself crossing the old causeway.

Suddenly there shot along the path a wild light, and I turned to see whence a gleam so unusual could have issued—for the vast house and its shadows were alone behind me.

The radiance was that of the full, setting, and bloodred moon, which now shone vividly through that once barely discernible fissure of which I have before spoken as extending from the roof of the building, in a zigzag direction to the base.

While I gazed, this fissure rapidly widened—
there came a fierce breath of the whirlwind—the entire orb
of the satellite burst at once upon my sight—my brain reeled
as I saw the mighty walls rushing asunder—there was a long
tumultuous shouting sound like the voice of a thousand waters—
and the deep and dank tarn at my feet closed sullenly and silently
over the fragments of the House of Usher.